monday
morning®

Boundless
Imagination

By Jan Thurman-Veith
Illustrated by Corbin Hillam

DEDICATION

for my mother
who taught me how
to love all
of life

ACKNOWLEDGEMENT:
Special thanks to Bee Huestis and Dave Simon
for their countless hours and treasured friendship

Publisher: Roberta Suid
Editor: Elizabeth Russell
Design and Production: Susan Pinkerton
Cover art: Corbin Hillam

monday morning ®

Monday Morning is a registered trademark
of Monday Morning Books, Inc.

ISBN 0-912107-55-3

Printed in the United States of America

9 8 7 6 5 4 3 2 1

Contents

Introduction

The magic of imagination is in every child. As parents and teachers, we can share in the discovery of this magic by opening doors to new ideas. Here we find the possibility for endless learning adventures through creative experiences and play.

Boundless Imagination offers activities that unleash creativity by filling the senses and instilling a true fascination for learning. Among the easy-to-do but powerful experiences are:

- creating an imaginary creature
- pretending to be a balloon
- making up dizzy directions
- dancing at an ugly bug ball
- attending an *un*birthday party
- dressing-up as visitors from space

As you try these simple games and projects, you will have opportunities to share in some of childhood's most memorable moments.

Under the best circumstances, imagination comes naturally to young children. There are no rules to follow nor patterns to copy. Right or wrong answers have nothing to do with it. All that's needed are fun-filled experiences that challenge the whole child. When carefully structured, such experiences enhance the child's understanding of the world, of cooperation, and of learning.

EXPLORING THROUGH PLAY

Unfortunately, the natural access to imagination can easily be blocked. A growing number of children, bombarded by expensive toys and weaned on television, no longer gain knowledge and insight through play. They have become passive rather than active learners.

This book is dedicated to helping you reverse this trend. For our children to become imaginative problem solvers and well-adjusted adults, we must give them opportunities to interact with each other.

It has been said many times that play is a child's work. Just watch a child's face during imaginative play. See the sheer delight of childhood at its best, learning at its peak with self-confidence soaring. As young children discover the wonders of everyday life, they have an eagerness and an openness to virtually everything. Their imaginations keep this tremendous energy alive.

CREATIVE LEARNING

The activities in this book were designed to encourage the *active* use of imagination in a positive learning environment. These proven activities are more likely to succeed if you keep a few basic ideas in mind:

- Get in touch with the child inside you and enjoy yourself.
- Maintain a warm and supportive rapport. Close relationships will heighten self-esteem and the spirit of friendship.
- Involve everyone. Shared and cooperative experiences give children a sense of value. Together they discover the joy of accomplishment.
- Grasp moments for teaching. Imaginative play allows each child to begin at his or her own level in the learning process.
- Encourage positive physical contact. It is important for children to touch for development of their sensory-motor systems.
- Believe in the power of imagination. Captivate young children with wide-eyed expressions and a twinkle in your eye.
- Be flexible. Remember, there are no rules. Modify any activity to make it work magically for you and your children.

ART

Create a Creature

Describe a troll, a monster, a hobbit — anything that the children have not seen before — in sharp detail from its head to its toes. Let the children make up a name for the creature. Then have them draw the creature as they see it in their mind's eye, without anyone else seeing. They can add funny features, silly clothing, and something likable about the creature to spark more of the imagination. When everyone has finished, share the pictures. No two creatures are alike because no two people and no two imaginations are alike.

Another way to describe the creature is to have the children take turns adding the characteristics until the creature is complete. This creature can be wild and woolly or silly and cute, but in the end, each child's creation will be unique.

Materials: paper and drawing tools

"An essential aspect of creativity is not being afraid to fail."

Edwin Land

Just a Clue

On a large piece of white paper, draw a few bold lines, a shape or two, a part of this or that, without actually having anything in mind. Prepare enough sheets to provide one for each child in the class. Give the children the papers and ask them to complete the pictures. If a child has difficulty, share another clue or offer another paper. The results of this creative project will be fascinating. If the children have a story, as they usually do, write it at the bottom of the paper. Remember that there is no right or wrong, only pure creativity and unquestionable success.

Materials: paper, crayons, pen

"The answers to life are not in the back of the book."

Dr. George Sheehan

Musical Portraits

Play wordless music — classical, jazz, big band, or children's melodies. Give each child a sheet of paper and a black crayon or marking pen. Ask the children to draw an illustration of the sounds, moving from one side of the paper to another. It is not necessary to create a line drawing. However, it often helps children to focus on the music rather than on making a picture. When complete, have the children "paint the music" by adding any form of abstract bold colors or blends to further illustrate the feelings of the music. Talk about how music makes a person feel. Listen to contrasting styles and compare drawings. What colors seem happy? What makes an illustration look scary or slow or fun?

Materials: music, paper, black crayons or markers, paint, and brushes

"One is never tired of painting, because you have to set down not what you know already, but what you have just discovered."

William Hazlitt

11

Mystery Art

Provide the children with artist's tools. Ask them to close their eyes while they draw — no peeking allowed! When the pictures are complete, the children open their eyes. Only then do they decide what it is they have drawn.

Materials: paper, paint, crayons or markers, aprons (optional)

"Of all people, children are the most imaginative."

Thomas Macaulay

Personal Puzzles

Take photographs of the children or use self-portraits they draw themselves. Cover each picture with clear contact paper and cut them into puzzle pieces. Let the children fit the pieces of their own and their friends' picture back together in a very personal puzzle experience.

*Using a child's own picture or self-portrait in a puzzle will add more meaning to the activity and give the child a better sense of self and body awareness.

Materials: photographs or self-portraits (done with crayons on paper), clear contact paper, scissors

"When I stopped seeing my mother with the eyes of a child, I saw the woman who helped me give birth to myself."

Nancy Friday

Pudding Painters

Mix or beat instant pudding and milk until creamy. Pour the mixture onto a clean or covered table surface. Have painters roll up their sleeves and begin their Picasso masterpieces, using both hands and all ten fingers as their paintbrushes. Cleanup is easy — just lick fingers clean! Try different flavors of pudding to add a variety of colors to the painters' palettes.

Materials: instant pudding mixes, milk

"All human beings have as their birthright the ability to be creative."

Albert C. Romano

Rorschach Art

Give each child a piece of white paper. Fold it one or two times. Let the children unfold it and drop on a small glob of paint. The children fold the paper again and press or flatten it. Open the paper and let the paint dry. Later, look at each picture and ask the children to imagine what it could be. Everyone will have a different idea. Turn the paper and look again. Now what does it look like? Turn again. What is it this time?

*This art experience is not only creative but also very good for developing divergent thinking skills in young children. The Rorschach test, devised by Hermann Rorschach, is a psychological tool in which a person's interpretations of abstract designs are analyzed as a measure of emotional and intellectual functioning and integration.

Materials: white paper, paint, cleanup supplies

"He who follows another sees nothing, learns nothing, seeks nothing."

Sir William Osler

Snake Painting

Instead of a brush, give the children string to paint with. Tell them how a snake crawls and slides and coils up and stretches out as it moves along. Each child may have a separate piece of paper or the class make make a mural of snake painting with snake tracks of different colors.

Materials: string, paint, paper

"The final purpose of the arts is pleasure."

G.E. Lessing

Stencil Stamps

Cut patterns from potatoes to create an infinite number of stencil art projects. Simply cut out the shapes with a knife, then dip the shape into a shallow pan of paint that is not too wet. It's a good idea to experiment on paper first. Then press the pattern onto fabric or paper. Repeat to make a border. Use a variety of colors, if desired.

Materials: potatoes, shallow pan, paint, fabric or paper, cleanup supplies

"Children are the keys to paradise."

R.H. Stoddard

Stick Drawings

Have the children pose in any position they like. Draw a stick figure of each one on a large sheet of paper. Then let them see the drawings and guess which one represents their pose. The next time, give them a stick figure drawing and let them put their bodies into that position, or you can be a stick figure and let them draw you. Help them realize that your arms or legs are up or out or both on one side. Let them draw a stick figure, and you can try to assume that position — fun and creative art for everyone!

*This activity also gives children a sense of their bodies in space and perceptual awareness for drawing what they see in a very simple form.

Materials: paper, crayons

"Great actions speak of great minds."

John Fletcher

DRAMA

And Sew On . . .

Give each child an imaginary needle and thread. Have everyone thread the imaginary needle slowly and carefully, pulling the thread through and tying a knot at the end. Push the needle through one finger, then the next, eventually "sewing" all fingers of the free hand. Next, have the children sew their own body parts together — hands to legs, knee to knee, and so on . . . When the thread is pulled, all the body parts pull tightly together. Keep sewing until nothing can move. *Help! Somebody get the scissors fast!*

"Good nonsense is good sense in disguise."

unknown

Body Puppets

Mouth Puppets: With fist turned so that thumb faces chest, use the opening as the puppet's big mouth. Apply red lipstick and mark eyes with a make-up pencil. The children may enjoy making both hands into puppets so they can have a conversation.

Toe Puppets: Draw eyes, nose, and mouth on big toes. Put feet up and wiggle toes to gesture. There's plenty to talk about. . . *those shoes were so tight and, whew, what about those smelly socks!*

Thumb Puppets: Thumbs up and faces on! Thumb people can have many adventures. With the help of arms, they can travel up and down mountains, staircases, even a giant's leg. Close fingers around them so they can go inside houses, caves, or spaceships. Open hand like a door and let thumb peek out of a window. Thumbs can run, hop, and lie down. What else?

Knee Puppets: Drape yarn, paper, or a wig over the top of the knee to make a knee puppet with a funny look. Draw on a matching face and have a visit with the next-knee neighbor!

Materials: lipstick, make-up pencil, yarn, paper, or wigs for hair

"It will be gone before you know it. The fingerprints on the wall will appear higher and higher. Then suddenly they disappear."

Dorothy Evslin

Car Wash

Run the children through an imaginary car wash. First, drive up (crawl or ride) to fill up gas tanks and have windshields cleaned (glasses or goggles sprayed with a mister bottle, then wiped with a sponge). Then move through the spray and scrub (hand mixer with strips of thin cloth tied to the beater). Now move on to the dryer, and finally to the cash register to pay for the sparkling clean wash! Everyone will want many turns to be both the cars and the car-washers. One time they may drive through in a car, the next time in a truck, and the next time in a big bus! Give the children some ideas for enrichment, such as, "Uh oh, better put the antenna down!" "Don't forget to turn off the engine!" "Little extra shine on those wheels, Miss?"

Materials: glasses or goggles, spray bottle filled with water, small sponge, mixer with strips of cloth tied to beater

Wash the car
Make it shiny and bright.
Start with the windshield
And then do the lights.

Get it all wet
From the front to the back.
Scrub it, dry it,
And that's that!

"If you enjoy the work you do, then you are one of the lucky few."

Charles Osgood

Circus Circus

Tightrope Walker: Blindfold the children and have them take off their shoes. Lay out a rope on the floor in straight lines and curves. Let the children walk the "tightrope" with their arms out, feeling very carefully with their toes. Follow the tightrope along all of its curves.

Tiger Through the Hoop: Spin a hula hoop backward very hard and fast to make it stay upright and return. The "tigers" leap or dive through the hoop onto a mat. Hold the hoop steady for younger children, if desired.

Clowns: Children roll in somersaults, play leap-frog, and make funny faces.

Tattoo People: Use water paints to make tattoos on arms, legs, and faces. Show off by parading around the circus ring.

Materials: blindfold, rope, hoop, map, baggy pants, big shoes, colorful wigs, garden gloves, lipstick and make-up pencils for clown faces, water paints, clean-up towels.

"Anyone who stops learning is old, whether at twenty or eighty. Anyone who keeps learning stays young. The greatest thing in life is to keep your mind young."

Henry Ford

Dog Gone

Everyone has an imaginary dog — purebred or mutt, big or small, vicious or friendly. Hook a collar around each dog's neck, and snap on the leash. Now take the dogs for a walk. Can the dog do any tricks? *Lie down. Roll over. Play dead. Heel. Good dog! Uh oh, the dog gets away. Dog gone!*

"Credulity is the man's weakness but the child's strength."

Charles Lamb

28

The Improv Palace

Here are ideas for easy improvisations which require only one word answers from quick-thinking children. This activity really expands vocabulary and nonverbal expression.

kiss	scream
sneeze	wiggle
cry	wave
lick	wink
pound	blink
pull	snap
bend	shudder
taste	spin
itch	jump
whistle	hop
chew	crawl

"Imitation is the sincerest form of flattery."

Charles Caleb Colton

Lion Safari

Take the children on an imaginary safari, complete with jungle sound effects and all kinds of jungle dangers. Seat the children on the floor and make appropriate gestures and noises as the story progresses.

We're going on a Lion Safari. Let's not forget our binoculars (hands cupped and held to eyes), cameras, and backpacks! I'm not afraid. Are you? (Noooo!) Bye, Mom! (Start walking by slapping hands alternately on lap.) Whew, it's hot (wipe forehead). What's that? A swamp? Tall, tall grass. Can't go under it, can't go over it . . . we'll have to go through it. Swish, swish, swish. Hey, a tree. Let's climb it. Hang onto the branch and look through your binoculars. Look up, look down, look all around. See any lions? (Make jungle noises.) Okay, climb back down — whee! Let's run. Hurry. Uh oh, a fallen tree. We can't go over it. We can't go around it. We'll have to go under it! (Get down close to the floor.) Oh, I made it. Did you?

"Who's ready for lunch? Let's have a look in our packs. I've got a peanut butter sandwich. And an orange! What do you have? Yum, yum. I'm thirsty. I see a river. (Walk over.) Scoop up a drink. Aah, cold water. Ouch, mosquitoes! (Slap cheeks.) Hey, we've got to get across the river. Can't go under it, can't go over it. We'll have to swim across it. (Kick, stroke, kick, stroke.) Shake off. Let's go. Yuck, it's muddy here. Schluck, schluck, schluck. Quicksand? Throw me a rope. (Pull hard!) Oh, saved! We've got to climb a tree and take another look. Look up, down, and all around. See a lion? No? Ssssh, uh oh, what's that? A snake! Jump down. Whew! Look ahead . . . a big mountain. Can't go over it, can't go under it. We'll have to go around it. Let's run. Whew, I'm tired (heavy sigh). Look ahead. (Whisper.) I think I hear something. Ssssh. Yikes! A lion! Take a picture. Click. Uh oh, run! Here he comes! (Go all the way back through every hazard of the trip.) Are you exhausted? Did you almost get caught? Did anyone lose their binoculars or camera? Let's go home and tell Mom. I wasn't afraid! Were you???"

*Create a new and exciting adventure for each Lion Safari. The children may warn you of the elephant stampede and point out the upcoming hazards. Beware!

"Sometimes I believed as many as six impossible things before breakfast."

Lewis Carroll

Lollipops

Show the children a big sack of imaginary lollipops and let them pick the color that they would like. *(Mmmmm. What flavor is yours? Mine is cherry.)* Take off the paper, crumple it up, and put it in your pocket, or carry it to the trash can. Start licking and tell this little story:

Some lollipops last a long, long time.
(Long, long licks very slowly between lines.)
You lick and lick and lick,
and then you keep on licking . . .
until . . . all . . . you . . . have
left . . . to lick . . . is the stick!

Uh oh, all gone. Throw your stick in the trash can and lick off your lips.

*This special treat is as good as any real sugar-filled, brightly colored, sweet-tasting lollipop. All it takes is some serious silliness!

"The less of routine, the more of life."

A. B. Alcott

32

Kings and Queens

The children take turns as king or queen, wear a crown and robe, and sit on a throne. The other children deliver messages. When the king or queen rings a bell, the first messenger stands up and gives his message through a megaphone. Messages can be true or false statements, such as "Red is a color," "My name is John," or "Elephants are little." If the statement is true, the king or queen nods yes. If it is untrue, the king or queen says no with a shake of the head.

*Help the first few messengers think of appropriate messages.

Materials: paper towel tube for megaphone, bell, paper crown, old bathrobe

"Before I got married I had six theories about bringing up children. Now I have six children and no theories."

Lord Rochester

Magic Carpet

Tell a story about how magic can make a carpet (an old sheet or blanket) fly. . . anywhere! Seat the children facing the same direction while flapping the ends of the sheet to give the carpet the magic lift to fly. *Hang on for the take-off! Whoa, over the clouds and up toward the sun. Can you find your house? Whee, where shall we go?* Land anywhere — in the zoo for a quick look at the giraffes, zebras, and elephants, or on the mountains to build a snowman, and even by the ocean to collect seashells. Then hurry back to the magic carpet for the trip home. *Hold on tight. Up, up, and away! Soon we land softly back on the floor in our room. What a magical adventure.*

Materials: old sheet or blanket for carpet

Magic carpet
Magic carpet
Take us away,
High in the air
For a very special day.

Where shall we go?
You may decide
To the mountains or the zoo?
Or for a wild ride?

"Imagination is more important than knowledge."

Albert Einstein

Mini-imagination Experiences

Make soundless gestures depicting a person doing something.

Playing with a yo-yo
Swatting a fly on your nose
Pounding nails
Sawing a board
Driving a car
Scratching an itch
Playing the piano
Jumping rope
Ballet dancing
Being a rag doll
Leading a band
Petting a dog
Rocking a baby

"Clothe an idea in words and it loses its freedom of movement."

Egon Friedell

The Monster Mash

The monster mash is a dance. Dancers twist and turn their toes on the floor like they're mashing potatoes. When monsters mash, it's a spirited smash! Spooky, creepy, ghoulish monsters can shake the night away in full monster make-up and monster madness.

Monster Make-up: Put a small amount of cold cream on the children's faces so that the make-up will be easy to remove. Apply face paints or water colors to create all sorts of mean monsters who will attend the scary affair. Turn down the lights, turn up the rock-'n-roll, and let the dancing begin.

*This may be a good time to talk about the difference between what is real and what is imaginary. Children should never be frightened by unreal things. Be sure that everyone knows that monsters are only creatures that are imagined for fun.

Materials: face cream, paints or make-up pencils, monster party clothes, music

"Worry is imagination misplaced."

Jim Fiebig

37

Old Time Favorites

Little Miss Muffet Let two children act out this nursery rhyme. Little Miss Muffet will need a frilly hat, an imaginary bowl and spoon, and a chair. That scary spider will need only a good imagination.

Humpty Dumpty: Put Humpty up on a sofa or bed and let him fall into pillows below. Send the king's horses and men to try to put him together in one piece again. *No way? Poor Humpty, he was a good egg.*

Snow White and the Seven Dwarfs: If there are more than eight children, add as many dwarfs as necessary. Think of extra names. (Snoozy? Skippy? Sneaky?) The children will enjoy choosing their characters and deciding on their own personalities. Do two children want to be Snow White? Okay, she was a twin. Be flexible and creative.

Three Little Kittens: Add whiskers with a make-up pencil and use real or imaginary mittens. Be sure to encourage the children to use their special voices to scold or praise those forgetful kittens.

Three Bears: Using different voices makes this story even more fun — Papa Bear with his deep, gruff voice, Mama Bear with her calm but concerned voice, and of course, Baby Bear with his little whining voice. Use objects to represent the bowls (coins or caps), beds (tissues or boxes) and chairs (lids or buttons), or have the children draw the props with crayons on paper or with chalk on the sidewalk.

Little Red Riding Hood: Find something red for the Little Red Riding Hoods to wear. Have the children make masks for the wolves and hats for the grandmas.

Three Pigs: There can be four, five, or more pigs and a pack of wolves, if necessary. Use some kind of shelter for the houses — chairs, a table on its side, pillows piled up, etc. If you have an audience, encourage them to boo and hiss and warn the little piggies to run when the wolf comes. They can also help huff and puff and provide other sound effects. If you have more than three pigs, let them tell you what their house is made of. In the end, be sure to have the wolf run away and never come back — that is, until next time. Let's not do anything cruel to the wolf, since wolves can be friends, too.

"To enjoy life in this world, one must always deal with people, never with things."

Galiani

39

Peanut Butter Lipstick

Give each child a small cup filled with peanut butter and a wooden craft stick or tongue depressor. In front of a mirror, the children put on the "lipstick." Smile . . . oh, how pretty! Then the lipstick can be licked off for no-hands clean-up.

Materials: small cups, peanut butter, wooden craft sticks or tongue depressors, mirror

> Peanut butter lipstick
> Would you like a kiss?
> I put it on
> then lick it off,
> around and around,
> and up and down.
> Mmmmmmmmwhaaaaaaa
> A kiss you wouldn't miss!

"Laughter is the sensation of feeling good all over and showing it principally in one place."

Josh Billings
(Henry Wheeler Shaw)

40

Poor Old Pete

One child is "Poor Old Pete" and sits in a chair in front of the others. Tell the children a story about a man whose body is falling apart. When he tries to brush his teeth, his hand falls off. When he wants to kiss his wife, his lips fall off.

Since Poor Old Pete obviously needs some help, have the children tape his broken-down body back together. *What is falling off now? His ear? Okay, better put a piece of tape on his ear to hold it on. His nose? Yes, it certainly is. Tape it on for Poor Ole Pete. His ankle? His toe? His tummy? His hair? It's lucky Pete has all these friends to put him back together. Is he all fixed up now? Hooray for old Pete!*

*This can be a funny story about any child in the group — not just Poor Old Pete. The next time, tell the children that he was kicking a ball. Ask them, *"What fell off? Yes, his foot!"* Or, for more imagination and language development, have the children tell you what Poor Old Pete was doing and what body part was falling off.

41

Race Car Drivers

Give each child a steering wheel made from a paper plate with triangular cut-outs. Everyone sits in a "driver's seat." Be sure to fasten seat belts! Start the cars, turn on the lights, and take off on a wild ride. Encourage sound effects of the roaring engines. Guide the children through the ride: veer left, make a quick right, stop at the traffic light, watch out for the roadblock, and avoid the oncoming cars. Drive carefully and get home safely!

Materials: paper plates for steering wheels, chairs, material for seat belts (optional)

"The life of the laws has not been logic; it has been experience."

Oliver Wendell Holmes, Jr.

Shaving Just Like Daddy

Give each child a small cup full of "shaving cream" (whipped cream) and a "razor" (craft stick). Looking into a mirror, the children put the shaving cream on their faces, all over their imaginary beards and mustaches. Then, slowly and carefully, they "shave" off their whiskers until they can feel their smooth faces. Next time they can give someone else a shave.

*Be sure the children understand that *real* razors are not to play with.

> Put on the cream
> You can have a taste
> Now shave it off carefully
> And make a funny face!

Materials: whipping cream, mixer, bowl, small cups, crafts sticks or tongue depressors, mirror

"My mother loved children — she would have given anything if I had been one."

Groucho Marx

43

Silly Sally

Silly Sally is a little girl who always gets mixed up. *Do you ever get things backwards? Well, Silly Sally was so silly that one day she was getting ready for school, and she put her pants on her arms! (Put pant legs on as sleeves.) Yes, and she put her gloves on her toes. And then she put her shirt around her knees. And her socks on her hands. And her scarf around her ankles! Wasn't she silly! But last of all, she was so silly that she put her lipstick on her chin. Oh my, what a mess she was. He mother came in and said, "Oh, Silly Sally, you're so silly! Your scarf goes . . ." (let children redress you), and "Your socks go . . ." etc.*

Next time, use the name of a child in your group (Silly Billy?), and dress him or her as you tell the silly story.

Materials: funny-looking hats, pants, skirts, shoes, gloves, socks, scarves, make-up and lipstick.

"The one serious conviction that a man should have is that nothing is to be taken too seriously."

Samuel Butler

44

Uh Oh's

Set out a doctor's table. The children will probably know the doctor's routine fairly well. They will listen to each other's hearts, examine sore throats, take temperatures, and almost always give lots of shots. Be the patient yourself and let the children know your fears. Is it going to hurt?

Go in with a broken leg. Tell a doctor of your skiing accident or your fall down the stairs. A nurse will surely comfort you and assure you that you'll feel better soon. Let a doctor put a cast on your leg with a roll of toilet paper wrapped around and around. Let the medical staff apply band-aids to their patients' many "uh-oh's." And don't leave without your prescription!

Materials: table, chairs, toilet paper, band-aids or masking tape, tongue depressors, paper and pencil, flashlight, toy doctor kit (optional)

"The art of medicine consists of amusing the patient while nature cures the disease."

Voltaire

Watch the Wizards

Fill a bag with pictures of animals. Have the children make wizard hats (black construction paper wrapped in a cone shape and stapled with stars or stickers attached) and magic wands (pencils with foil-covered tips). Tie plastic liners loosely around their necks for capes, and they become powerful wizards.

Everyone says the magic chant:

It's magic. It's magic.
Wait and see!
It's magic. It's magic.
What will YOU be?

Then the first wizard waves the magic wand (carefully) and reaches into the bag for a picture and . . . abracadabra, whoosh! The other children become the animal! Encourage expressions of the animal. Help the children get involved in their roles — hissing snakes, growling lions, playful kittens.

Now let the children do magic tricks. For example, close your eyes so they can make things disappear. Or, with a swirl of their wands, they can make a friend jump, spin, or go down the slide. What magical fun! And don't forget the magic chant!

Remember to turn the wizards back into children!

Materials: bag, pictures of animals, construction paper, stapler, stars, pencils and foil, black plastic trash can liners

"There is no meaning to life except the meaning man gives his life by the unfolding of his powers."

Erich Fromm

Who Did It? "I Dunno!"

Invite one child to be "I Dunno." Since I Dunno is invisible, he is always getting in the way and getting into trouble. "I dunno" will have to be painted bright colors so that people can know what he's up to every minute. Where to start? Let the children choose the imaginary colors they want to use. What color should the arms be? Red? Who has red? Now the hands. Continue painting (with water, of course) until "I Dunno" is completely covered. Watch out, though. When the paint wears off, there will be trouble again. *Who did it? I dunno! Not me!*

I Dunno is in trouble
Whether he likes it or not.
He leaves the doors open
And the lights on a lot.
He knocks down things
That crash on the floor.
I Dunno does all that —
And much more!

I'd like to catch him
Just once in the act,
So when they ask me
I'll tell them . . .
Who did that?
I Dunno!

48

MUSIC AND MOVEMENT

"Air Band" Rock-'n-Rollers

Find a record or tape of popular songs that use many different instruments (drums, guitars, horns piano, etc.). Give each child an imaginary instrument. Set up the stage and turn on the music. Everyone strums, drums, blows, or plays along (and dancers are welcome, too). Turn off the lights and use a flashlight for special "spotlight" effects.

*Children love music! This activity gets them involved and helps them develop a sense of rhythm and beat.

Materials: music, flashlight (optional)

"I haven't understood a bit of music in my life, but I have felt it."

Igor Stravinsky

Balloon-A-Foolery

After the children decide what color balloons they will be, have them lie flat on the floor as uninflated balloons. Using a real balloon, blow in a small amount of air while the children begin to "fill up." Blow (they're getting bigger), blow (bigger still), blow (standing up), blow (reaching out). *Oh, can the balloon hold any more air? A little more? Blow — ooh, it's about to pop!* Then pop the balloon with a pin, and the children fall to the floor and lie still.

Next time, blow the balloon up bigger and bigger until it's nice and round — then let it go! The children twist and spin and finally fall to the floor.

> I'm a (red/blue/green) balloon
> As flat as can be.
> I'm getting bigger, bigger
> And bigger as you can see.
> Bigger and bigger . . . will I pop?
> Let the air out — SSSSSSSSSS.
> Now I stop.

Materials: pin, large balloons (have several — the children will want to do this over and over again!)

Boa Constrictor

One child stands with both feet inside a fabric "snake." Sing the "Boa Constrictor" song (by Peter, Paul, and Mary) from Shel Silverstein's *Where the Sidewalk Ends*. As the song is sung, the boa constrictor swallows the child's toes (making slurping and munching noises), then the child's knees *(mmm, good)*, then the child's middle, neck, and then — *slurp* — the snake swallows the child whole! How will the child get out? *A burp? Oh my!*

Simply wrap your arms around the child and squeeze as the boa constrictor "gulps" if you do not wish to make the fabric snake.

Materials: two pillow cases or a sheet sewn to make a long tube (add eyes or a felt-covered cardboard snake's head to the top edge, if desired)

"It is almost as important to know what is not serious as to know what is."

John Kenneth Galbraith

Dirty Laundry

The children take turns as imaginary washing machines. "Sort" the other children according to the colors that they're wearing, so that those wearing red go into one pile, those wearing white go into another pile, and so on. The child who is the washing machine stands up. The other children waiting to be washed lie in piles nearby. Add imaginary soap and push the start button. The washing machine begins to "agitate" back and forth, while the laundry rocks and moves freely. Then the rinse water shoots in (make sounds "ssshhhhshshsh"), and the laundry stops and floats. When the washing machine drains, the spin cycle starts. Watch out! The agitator spins around and around while the clothes lie flat. Then it's done. Take the laundry out and throw it into the dryer, where it tumbles and rolls until it is all dry (and tired).

*If this activity is too complicated for some children, let everyone be the agitator, and then the clothing in the dryer. Be sure the children experience watching a washing machine before they become one.

54

This is the way we sort our clothes,
Sort our clothes, sort our clothes.
This is the way we sort our clothes,
So early in the morning.

This is the way we wash our clothes...

This is the way we spin our clothes...

This is the way we dry our clothes...

"Nothing is more terrible than activity without insight."

Thomas Carlyle

Drill Team

Tie or tape a strip of crepe paper or a piece of ribbon to the end of a pencil or dowel. Have the children march in place while twirling their "flags" overhead and in front of their bodies (caution them to be careful of their neighbors). Then line the children up and march with the full drill team or let them move about freely.

Materials: tape, crepe paper or ribbon, pencils or dowels, marching band music (optional)

"When children are doing nothing, they are doing mischief."

Henry Fielding

Finger Ballet

Using the index and middle fingers as "legs," the "dancers" limber up on the dance floor (table), stretching, bending, and jumping. Play some classical music and watch as the finger ballet dancers execute their leaps, turns, and plies. Everyone should join in for the Great American Dance Company's finest performance.

Materials: classical music

Giant's Sandwich

Create a delicious sandwich big enough to feed a giant, using two mats for bread slices and many scrumptious children for the filling. Ask the giant what kind of sandwich he or she would like for lunch today — peanut butter and jelly? Okay, hold open one slice of bread and fill with children. Close the sandwich and . . . wait, oh no, here come the ants (the rest of the children), crawling right over the giant's sandwich. (Be sure the children are lying flat and the ants crawl only over their bodies, not their heads.) Here comes the giant! The ants run away as fast as they can, and the giant gobbles up the leftovers. Still hungry, Mr. Giant? How about tuna? Egg salad? Bacon and tomato? Let's make another one!

*Being inside the sandwich provides a great deal of sensory stimulation from the pressure of the ants climbing over the mats. Most children love this feeling, but don't hesitate to let a child out who is uncomfortable.

Materials: mats

"Sweet childish days, that were as long as twenty days are now."

William Wordsworth

Goin' on the Bus

Form a bus with chairs set up in a line with wheels on the sides. Each child may have a steering wheel. Collect imaginary tickets and find out where everyone is going. Sing the "People on the Bus" song, making up new verses about the passengers on this bus:

The kids on the bus were waving to their friends...
>   (clapping their hands)
>   (brushing their hair)
>   (whistling a tune)

Materials: chairs, steering wheels made from paper plates

"Your sole contribution to the sum of things is yourself."

Frank Crane

59

Human Bowling Pins

Put small pieces of masking tape on the floor to mark the usual triangular arrangement of bowling pins and an alley. Position the children as "human bowling pins," standing rigidly with their arms at their sides and their feet together. Use a foam, yarn, or other soft ball. Stand back, aim, and roll the ball down the alley. *Pow!* The pins fall down if the ball touches them. How many pins are left standing? Try for a spare. *Oops, gutter ball.* Count your score. The pins stand up, and the bowlers are ready for the next frame.

For extra fun, have the pins roll to the side before resetting them — just like at the bowling alley! Or let the children bowl, and become a pin yourself.

*You can also make bowling pins by filling quart-size milk cartons one-third full of sand and stapling the tops closed. Use a heavier ball to knock these pins down.

> All the bowling pins
> Standing up tall.
> I'm looking and aiming
> And — rolling the ball . . .
>
> POW! The pins fall down
> Here and there.
> Are there any still up?
> I'll try for a spare.

Materials: tape, soft ball; milk cartons, sand, stapler, ball (optional)

"Imagination is not the talent of some men but is the health of every man."

Ralph Waldo Emerson

Log Rolling

All children lie flat, shoulder to shoulder, on the floor. Now they become long, heavy, rigid logs that must get down the conveyor belt. With arms stiff and held tightly to the body, legs straight, the end log begins to roll. Bodies must stay rigid so that knees and elbows don't hurt anyone. As the log rolls up and over the log jam, it falls into place, fitting in tightly at the end. (Assist as necessary.) Then the next log begins, and the next, and the next. When all the logs reach the mill, the big saw starts to buzz. Zzzzzzzzzz. Quick, roll back!

*The children will squeal with anticipation of rolling or being rolled over. It is a wonderful sensory experience for them to feel pressure and weight and to develop body control.

"We are all here for a spell, get all the good laughs you can."

Will Rogers

Magical Musical Chairs

Form a circle of chairs, enough so that there is one chair for each child. Choose music with a strong and steady beat. As the music starts, the children walk around the chairs. When the music stops, they sit quickly in the nearest chair. Everyone has one. Now take one chair away and try it again. This time when the music stops, the child without a chair becomes *invisible* and sits on someone's lap! The game continues until there is only one chair left with everyone sitting on it!

*The rules of Magical Musical Chairs ensure that no one is left out after the game begins. No losers! This way everyone will experience success and have fun. Encourage the children to hang on to each other (attach "seatbelts"). When they sit on you, "groan" at how heavy they are. Sit on them (lightly) and they will squeal with delight!

> Our hands go clap
> Our feet go tap
> Around and around . . .
> then sit on a chair
> on somebody's lap!

Materials: music, chairs

Silly Songs

Make up verses to old favorite songs — the sillier the better. Here are some ideas.

She'll Be Coming Around the Mountain:

We'll be riding pink chimpanzees...
We'll be eating purple pancakes...
We'll be wearing peanut butter and jelly...

Skip to My Lou: Change the "skip" in each verse to jump, clap, snap, hop, etc.

If You're Happy and You Know It:

If you're tall...stand up!
If you're funny...give a grin!
If you're sleepy...start to snore!

Where is Thumbkin?: Use a child's name and let him or her pop up. Then shake hands as you ask, "How are you today, (child's name)?" He or she says, "Very well, thank you" and then runs away.

Old McDonald:

Mrs. _____ had a class, or
Mr. _____ had some kids,

Eeii, Eeii, Ooooo.

And in her class (his house) was
_____ named _____.

Eeii, Eeii, Oooooo.

With a boy and girl here,
And a boy and girl there,
Here a boy, there a girl,
Everywhere a boy and girl . . .

"All the fun is in how you say a thing."

Robert Frost

Snake Charmers

Find a container large enough for a child to sit in as the snake. Wrap a towel around another child's head as a turban, and use a piped instrument or simple vocal tones as an imaginary flute to "charm" the snake.

One child huddles inside the basket until the snake charmer begins the song. The mesmerized snake rises slowly, reaching out and waving back and forth gently with sounds of the flute. Finally the snake sinks back into the basket until charmed again or removed to his cage. Take turns.

Materials: basket or large container, towel or fabric, instrument (optional)

"It's easy to complain about children. But when we want to express our joy, our love, the words elude us. The feelings are almost so sacred they defy speech."

Joan McIntosh

Tickle/Hug Machine

Sit with palms out as "buttons" for either tickles or hugs. Draw a smile on the left hand for tickles and a heart on the right had for hugs. When a child pushes a button, the machine goes to work giving tickles or warm hugs. Only for a minute, though — everyone will want a chance to enjoy this one!

*Save this activity for the end of the day. Give out tokens during the day for the children to "cash in" for the Tickle/Hug Machine.

Or make a Tickle Tunnel by having the children kneel in two lines, facing each other. One child at a time crawls through quickly while the others reach out and tickle. This is pure tickle madness!

"If a child lives with approval, he learns to live with himself."

Dorothy Law Nolte

Upside-Down Bicycle Trip

Children lie on their backs, feet up, because this is an upside-down bicycle trip. Say, "Bye, Mom. See you later!" Climb on the bikes and start pedalling, looking at the trees and flowers alongside the road. *Uh oh, there's a big hill ahead . . . ugh, it's getting harder and harder to push. Keep going, we're almost to the top. Whew, we made it. Now let's's coast down very fast. WHEE!*

Hey, there's the ice cream man. Let's try to catch him. Faster, faster! Oh boy, he's stopping. We can slow down now and get off our bikes. Give him our money and . . . mmmmm. Lick, lick, lick. Back on our bikes now and head for home.

*During the ride, have the children describe in detail the sights of their own neighborhoods . . . ride by their friends' houses, wave to Mom and Dad, watch out for that dog that's chasing you, see all of the favorite "hot spots" — be spontaneous. The children will join in, and you'll be pedalling to keep up.

Bye, Mom,
Bye, Dad.
This is the silliest time
I've ever had.
Goin' on a bicycle trip
Upside down,
Pedalling my bike
All over town.

"Ever change your thoughts and you change your world."

Norman Vincent Peale

Wind-Up Toys

Turn an imaginary key on the back of each of the children to get them moving. When they unwind, they stop and "freeze," staying rigid until they are wound up again.

"You can't turn back the clock. But you can wind it up again."

Bonnie Prudden

STORYTELLING

Baking and Eggs

Read the children the story *Green Eggs and Ham* by Dr. Seuss. Then make green eggs and ham by adding a few drops of blue food coloring (since eggs are yellow) to scrambled eggs with bits of ham. While cooking, keep asking the children, "Would you like to eat it? No? You don't like green eggs and ham??? Would you, could you on a . . . ?" Then finally, try them. Mmmmm . . . We like green eggs and ham!

*This is a great way to learn that it is necessary to try new things to know if they're good.

Materials: eggs, ham, blue food coloring, frying pan

"What I want to do is to make people laugh so that they'll see things seriously."

William K. Zinsser

Bring and Brag

Everyone enjoys Show and Tell. This activity is much the same, except that the shared object is invisible. Let the children display whatever they dream up (but if it bites, it has to stay in its cage). Take turns telling all about the favorite "thing," whatever it may be. *What is it? Where did it come from? Where do you keep it? Does it eat much? Oh my!*

"If you want to see what children can do, you must stop giving them things."

Norman Douglas

Dizzy Directions

Have the children take turns inside a "tourist booth." From there they give detailed directions to wherever you're going — Disneyland, Mars, Kansas City, etc. Be sure to take notes so you won't make a wrong turn or miss a landmark. Have a good trip! Next!

If the children need prompting, help by asking them questions such as, "Do I have to go over any mountains?" or "After the white house, do I turn right or left?" or "What will I see before I cross the bridge?"

*This activity will help to improve the children's sense of directionality, laterality, space, numbers, distance, and time.

Materials: table, box or structure for tourist booth, paper and pencil

"All our knowledge has its origins in our perceptions."

Leonardo da Vinci

Guess Who's Coming!

Light a candle, turn down the lights, and tell this scary story:

Once there was an old, old woman who sat in a dark, dark house at the end of a long, long road. She sat spinning wool and rocking, waiting for someone to come. All of a sudden, there was a knock on the door (knock, knock, knock). The door opened slowly (creeeeeak), and in walked an ugly, ugly face (put cauliflower on a cookie sheet). But still the old woman sat and still she spun, and still she waited for someone to come. (Whisper.)

There was another knock on the door (knock, knock). In walked a long, crooked nose (add carrot) that sat right on top of the ugly, ugly face! But still the old woman sat and still she spun, and still she waited for someone to come.

Uh oh, another knock on the door. It opened (creeeeak), and in walked two big, black eyes (olives) that climbed up on the ugly, ugly face and sat down by the long, crooked nose. But still she sat, and still she spun, and still she waited for someone to come. And waited. And waited . . . until finally there was another knock on the door.

The door opened slowly (creeeeak), and in walked two green ears (bell peppers) that jumped up on the ugly, ugly face by the long, crooked nose and the big, black eyes. Another knock, and in came red, curly hair (red leaf lettuce) that sat on the top of the ugly, ugly face by the long crooked nose and the big, black eyes, and the green, green ears. But STILL the woman sat, and STILL she spun, and STILL she WAITED FOR SOMEONE TO COME!

Then there was a faint knock at the door (quiet knocking). The door creeeeeaked and in came some red, red lips (tomato slices) that went over and sat on the ugly, ugly face by the long, crooked nose and the big, black eyes and the green, green ears, and the red, curly hair. The old woman stopped spinning and stopped rocking, and the room was very quiet. . . (long, suspenseful pause). (Scream.) A witch! (Blow out the candle.) Then the old woman bit her nose off! (Bite off the end of the carrot.)

Ask if anyone would like to eat that mean old witch . . . mmm. Aren't those green, green ears and big, black eyes delicious!

*Let the children join in the preparation of the vegetables to gain valuable fine motor skills. Supervise closely! During this time, alert the children that you will be using this food to help tell a scary story. Should they be afraid? Nooooo. It's just for fun! They will surely enjoy the chance to gobble up this witchy treat.

Materials: toothpicks for attaching parts to face, cookie sheet, foil hat filled with black olives, cauliflower (carve hole to put carrot in), carrot, black olives, bell pepper slices, red leaf lettuce, tomato slices

"To talk to a child, to fascinate him, is much more difficult to win than an electoral victory. But it is more rewarding."

Colette

I Love You More Than . . .

This is a heartwarming interaction for any two people and a special favorite of children. Begin by telling someone, "I love you more than . . ." (name one of your favorite things). Then that child responds by saying "I love you more than . . ." and so on. The children will want to continue this loving exchange for hours.

Next time, begin with "I love you bigger than . . ." or "I love you wider than . . ." or "I love you higher than . . ."

"Once in a century a person may be ruined or made insufferable by praise, but surely once in a minute something dies for want of it."

John Masefield

Love Coupons

Help the children make coupons from strips of paper to give to someone they love. Each coupon is personal and may be redeemed for hugs, kisses, special time, big or little favors — almost anything the heart desires.

Materials: paper coupons, pencils

"Kindness in words creates confidence. Kindness in thinking creates profoundness. Kindness in giving creates love."

Lao-tzu

LOVE COUPONS

This coupon for_____
_____
to be given to_____
_____
from _____
with love. No limit to stock on hand. Offer good anytime. Value of coupon: Priceless.

Imagine That!

To begin, ask the children to close their eyes and keep them closed the whole time. Then ask them to imagine a little girl. She is standing in front of her house. *(Do you see her?)* She is wearing a red dress. *(See the girl in the red dress?)* She has a dog. He is wagging his tail. *(Do you see her dog? What kind of dog do you see?)* Oh, her mother is calling. *(Do you hear her mother? What is she saying?)* The little girl in the red dress runs into the house. *(Where is the dog? Is he still there?)* The door of the house opens and the little girl lets the dog go inside, too. *(Now what do you see?)* Just the house is there now. The end.

After practicing with visual imagery, have fun imagining silly things. Absurdity in the mind's eye is a never-ending source of laughter for young children. For example:

- an elephant riding a bicycle
- a boy sitting on the ceiling
- Daddy wearing a wig

*Visual imagery plays an important part in education. In learning, a child must be able to hold images for decision making, judgment, problem solving, and flexibility of thought.

"Where all think alike, no one thinks very much."

Walter Lippman

Magic Penny

Once there was a little boy named (child's name) who didn't have anything to do one day. He walked and walked, looking down at the ground because he felt sad and lonely. There, in the dirt, he saw something. He picked it up and brushed it off. What's this? It was shiny and round. It was a penny. And it was MAGIC! (Give each child a penny to look at, hold, and touch.) Each time he rubbed it, he got a wish! First, he wished for a friend. It was (child's name). They walked, holding hands, until they got hungry. They made another wish and got a big, red, juicy apple. Yummm. Can you rub your magic penny and make a wish?

*Using the children's names in the story will make it more interesting and exciting. Add many friends, or make the wishes something special to each particular child.

I found a penny
Today on the road.
If I rub it and shine it,
It may give me a wish of my own,
I'm told.

One Liners

Tell the children that the whole group is going to be involved in telling a story. It has a beginning, but it may continue on and on. The first child begins by telling one line of this tale. The second child adds a line. And the next child adds a line. You may want to keep the story line flowing by asking questions such as, "And what happened to the girl?" or "Oh, what will that man do now?!" Write the story, and later the children may want to illustrate it. The next day, continue the story or begin again.

Materials: paper and pencil, crayons for illustrations

"Self-doubt in the creative person can be removed by creative production."

Journal of Creative Behavior

Peculiar Pie

Use a big pot and spoon to mix the "ingredients" of this imaginary dessert. Decide what kind of pie it will be, choosing among such "flavors" as animals, vehicles, dinosaurs — anything. Then chant the musical rhyme below and clap along. At the end of the rhyme, a child pretends to put in one "ingredient." Stir it up, and taste it. *Does a truck go in a dinosaur pie? Noooo. It doesn't taste good. Does a tyrannosaurus go in a dinosaur pie? Yes? Mmmmm.* Sing again.

> Shake 'n bake
> Shake 'n bake
> What does the cook need to make . . .
> (Dinosaur Pie!)

When everyone has had a turn, add salt and pepper to taste and let everyone feast on this peculiar pie. *Yummm.*

Materials: pot, spoon

"When you are dealing with a child, keep all your wits about you, and sit on the floor."

Austin O'Malley

Ridiculous Recipes

Do you know how to prepare a turkey? To bake a delicious cherry pie? All you have to do is ask a child. Take note of the exact ingredients, cooking time, and oven temperature. These recipes can be collected and made into a cookbook by kids. It will tickle the tastebuds and be a delectible addition to anyone's cookbook collection.

CHOCOLATE CUPCAKES WITH WHITE FROSTING
by Josh (age 4)

    1 pile cheese
    5 quarters milk
    8 cups water (from faucet)
    2 flours
    Brown colors

Get it at the store. Put it in. Stir it around. and put it in that pan with holes. Cook it inside the stove for six hours at 9°. You know when it's finished because of the hills or the buzz goes off. Makes this many (three).

HOW TO COOK A DRAGON
by Samantha (age 4)

Cut it up.
Put salt on it.
Cook it 40 hours.
Then we look in the oven, and if it's all burnt up, we take it out and eat it. It tastes like chicken if you throw away the feathers.

Materials: paper, pen

"I am not young enough to know everything."

James M. Barrie

Secrets

Make up a secret language that sounds silly and is fun, too. Take a word like "boat." Drop the first sound and then add it to the end with "ay." It would become "oatbay." To say "dog," drop the "d" and add "day" at the end to get "ogday." Right? Now you say a word, and let's try to change it to the secret language. "Happy" would sound like "appyhay." Now guess what word this is: "igpay." Yes, pig!

Tell a story using key words that are in the secret language and watch the children listen like never before! For example:

Once there was an *eddybeartay* who lived in the forest. He was looking for a friend. One day he met an *abbitray*. He asked the *abbitray* if he would like to find a beehive and eat some honey. The *abbitray* said he didn't like honey. So the *eddybeartay* walked to the stream and met an *eerday*. He asked the *eerday* if she would like to catch some *ishfay* for lunch. The *eerday* said she only liked to eat grass and flowers. So finally the *eddybeartay* curled up and went to sleep. When he woke up he heard a funny sound. It was an *onkeymay*. He thought he had found a friend at last. He asked the *onkeymay* if he would like to climb a tree. The *onkeymay* said, "Oh yes!" and the *eddybeartay* and the *onkeymay* became the best of friends.

"Creativity is part of man's uniqueness."

Joseph Petrosky

Surprise Package

Give each child an imaginary surprise package, keeping one for yourself. Describe the wrapping, especially the bright colors and the fancy bow on the top. Have the children describe theirs in the same way. Now everyone opens the packages, taking off the paper, pulling off the tape, and the slowly removing the lid. Dig through the tissue paper and find your surprise. What did you find? What did everyone else find?

"Pleasure is the only thing to live for. Nothing ages like happiness."

Oscar Wilde

Tell-A-Kid Communications

The children sit in a large circle. Use paper cups connected with string for telephones. Have them pass verbal messages (short messages are best) from one to the next until the messages have traveled all the way around the circle. Have the last child say the message aloud. Was there a good connection on the line? Children never tire of this game, though the lines are sometimes "out of order!"

Materials: paper cups, string, scissors; tubes from paper towel rolls may be used instead of "telephones," and the children can whisper their messages to one another through the "transmitter"

"Playing as children means playing is the most serious thing in the world."

G.K. Chesterton

Unabashed Dictionary

Sit down with paper and pen for an eye-opening experience. Ask the children, one at a time and privately, to tell the meaning of certain words. Write the child's exact definition. Make these pages into a valuable reference book and priceless keepsake. The children may also help by making it a picture dictionary.

Select words that the children are not familiar with so that their imaginations will be hard at work as they provide the meanings. Try words like these: jitterbug, pessimist, exterminator, senator, Connecticut, usher, cabaret, oregano, prism, meteorologist, corporation.

Exterminator (by Lucas, age 4) That's what my Dad plays with in his car.

Prism (by Chelsea, age 3) Like this (twirls in the air). I know because I'm smart.

Litterbug (by Mario, age 3) Those ones that dig in the dirt. I eat one but my Mom said, "Yuck!"

Senator (by Joshua, age 3) My Mom bought me one at Toys R Us but my sister broke it. Now it doesn't do anything.

"Who knows the thoughts of a child?"

Nora Perry

Walkie Talkies

Separate the children into their own "stations" around the room. Then whisper a secret "order" to the child in Station 1. He or she delivers it to Station 2. The child in Station 2 delivers the message to Station 3, and so on. The last child to receive the secret information must carry out the order.

*Use orders that involve simple, concrete directions to help the children develop memory and listening skills. Make some of the orders silly and fun, too. Start the next message with the child in Station 2.

"Being a mother enables one to influence the future."

Jane Sellman

GAMES AND EVENTS

Bean Bag Mania

Make simple bean bags by sewing three sides of a fabric square. Leave one side open for the children to fill with beans. Write each child's name on the outside and let them decorate with felt markers or leave the fabric design plain. Fill and sew the end closed. The children will love to watch the sewing machine in action.

Use the bean bags for many imaginative games. For example:

- Toss the bags like popping corn.
- Use a spatula to flip the bags like pancakes.
- Knead the bags like dough for bread.
- Pass the bags quickly like hot potatoes.
- Throw the bags through someone's arms like shooting baskets through a hoop.

Materials: fabric, sewing machine, beans, markers (optional)

"Action! Action! Action!"

Demosthenes

Bouncing Balls

Drag a big imaginary bag of balls out of the closet. Take one ball out and hold it up. Feel its "roundness," bounce it, then toss it to one of the children. Take out some more balls and pass them around. They can bounce them, toss them back, or roll them around the room to the other children. Here comes one. Catch it!

"In every real man a child is hidden that wants to play."

Friedrich Nietzsche

Carousel

The children form a circle. Choose one child to be the leader, standing in the center, with ribbons or streamers reaching out to the other children. The circle of children moves around and up and down as galloping horse of the Merry-Go-Round.

To make a horse mask, place a paper bag over the child's head and mark the proper places for eyes. Remove the bag and cut out two holes for the eyes, them check to see if the child can see out of them when the mask is on. Let the child paint or color eyes, nose, and mouth. Fringed paper or other material can be glued on for the horse's mane. Ears can be cut out of paper, folded, and glued on.

Materials: ribbons or streamers cut in six-foot lengths, paper bags, scissors, paint or crayons, paper, glue

"There may be more beautiful times: but this one is ours."

Jean Paul Sartre

Gingerbread People

The children are the ingredients of these cookies. In an imaginary bowl, mix together one child as the flour, another as the sugar, another as the ginger, and so on. Stir up the ingredients, and the children will roll, curl up, and finally crowd together into a big ball of dough. Use a rolling pin to roll out the dough until it is flat, slowly pressing and rolling to each child's body. Cut out the gingerbread cookies by tracing around each child's body with your finger. Go up one arm to the shoulder and neck, around from one ear to the other, and then back around until the outline is complete. As the children are "baked," they act out feeling warm and puffed up. Oh, what sweet smells! When the cookies are done, the children come alive and run away! Try to catch the gingerbread cookies!

*Make real cookies so that the children understand the baking process. Let them form the cookies with their hands instead of using cookie cutters. Use this opportunity to tell the children the story of "The Gingerbread Man."

Gingerbread, gingerbread,
Gingerbread man,
Make me some cookies
As fast as you can.
Roll 'em, cut 'em,
And put 'em in the pan.
Bake 'em, smell 'em,
But. . .wait,
Watch out!
He'll run away if he can!

"You can do anything with children if you only play with them."

Prince Otto von Bismarck

Gingerbread Cookie Recipe

Ingredients:

- 1 cup shortening
- 1 cup sugar
- 1 egg
- 1 cup molasses
- 2 T vinegar
- 5 cups sifted all-purpose flour
- 1½ tsp. baking soda
- ½ tsp. salt
- 1 T ginger
- 1 tsp. cinnamon
- 1 tsp. cloves

Directions: Cream shortening with sugar. Add egg, molasses, and vinegar and beat well. Sift dry ingredients and stir in. Chill three hours.

Roll thin on lightly floured surface. Form shapes. Place one inch apart on greased cookie sheet. If desired, sprinkle with sugar. Bake in moderate over (375° F.) for five to six minutes. Cool slightly, then remove to rack to cool.

Lucky Leprechauns

Share the story of the wonderful little leprechauns, their magical powers and their joyful life in the woods. Describe their pointed ears, toes, and hats. Their favorite color is green. Did you know that leprechauns are the same size as children?

The day before St. Patrick's Day, leave a bag of gifts for the leprechauns. Everyone should find something green to put in the special sack. The next day, the sack is empty, but there are lots of little footprints on the floor leading out the door. Have the children follow the footprints and keep a close lookout for the little leprechauns. Do you see one? Finally, the footsteps lead to a pot of rainbow colors...gifts from the leprechauns to the children.

If time allows, let the children make their own leprechaun tracks. Put green paint with a few squirts of detergent (for easy clean-up) in a shallow pan. Have the children step in barefoot and make footprints across butcher paper or newspapers. Have soapy suds in a pan at the end of the line to clean the little green feet.

Materials: sack, footprints from paper or chalk, treats in rainbow colors (fruit, sugarless treats, balloons, stickers, etc.); green paint, detergent, pan, butcher paper or newspaper (optional)

Merry Melodies

Have musical instruments available. Invite one or more children to choose an instrument. They stand up and play, facing the others who are listening. Clap and say the musical rhyme below. At first there may simply be a lot of "noise," but the children will soon begin playing together and will enjoy listening to the concert. To end the song, give the orchestra members a round of applause. Form a new orchestra and play a new song.

> Play a tune
> Or a melody,
> A sweet little song
> Or a symphony!

Materials: musical instruments

"I'll play it first and tell you what it is later."

Miles Davis

Obstacle Course

Use all available furniture, mats, tables, and chairs to set up a course for the children. Station "guards" at selected points who require a password before moving aside. For example, the guard at the bridge would require the children to give the password "over." The guard at the tunnel would require the password "through," and so on. Or have the children go through the course blindfolded (for more sensory awareness). *Are you crawling through the desert? Are you mountain goats? Are you little ants following each other home?*

Materials: various types of furniture and equipment

"The best way out of a difficulty is through it."

unknown

People Puzzles

Make a very large shape on the floor with masking tape. It's fun to make letters and numbers. One by one the children fit their bodies along the outlined shape until the puzzle is complete. Let some children watch as the people puzzle comes to life.

Materials: masking tape

"An educated person gets his ideas from someone else. An intelligent person creates his own ideas."

unknown

Purple Hearts Ceremony

Have your group recognize heroic deeds or displays of bravery and courage by awarding purple hearts. Let the recipient recreate the heroic act for the whole group. Pin the purple heart on the child's chest with a safety pin and end the ceremony with a round of applause.

*Bravery is a part of every child's day, whether it involves passing by the big dog on the corner, surviving a crash on a bicycle and a skinned knee, or smiling through a visit to the dentist. A child's ability to cope with and adjust to life's ongoing challenges requires a lot of courage!

Materials: purple hearts cut from paper, safety pins

"The hunger for applause is the source of all conscious literature and heroism."

Duc de La Rochefoucauld

Sneaky Simon

Although Sneaky Simon tells us what to do (like his cousin Simple), watch out! He may tell us to touch our toes, but sometimes he touches his nose! He may tell us to clap our hands, but sometimes he stamps his feet! Encourage the children to listen very carefully and do only what he says, not what he does. He's sneaky, but don't let him trick you!

*This activity develops critical listening skills. Since children rely primarily on what they see rather than on what they hear, Sneaky Simon helps them focus on listening in an enjoyable way.

"The unexpected always happens."

Lawrence J. Peter

Space Balls

UFOs: Poke colored toothpicks into the skin of an apple or orange. Use grapes or raisins on the toothpicks for UFOs.

Scrumptious Space Spheres:

1 cup crushed graham crackers
1 cup non-fat dry milk
1 cup corn syrup
1 cup crunchy peanut butter
½ cup raisins
½ cup chopped walnuts
½ cup wheat germ

Add dry milk to crackers. Stir in corn syrup. Add peanut butter and the rest of the ingredients. Form small balls and chill.

Space Invaders

Build a spaceship with sheets and blankets draped over chairs or tables, and add whatever objects are available in the room as instruments and equipment. Hang foil "stars" from the ceiling and foil-covered balloons to represent constellations and other planets. Cover the floor with open egg cartons, Styrofoam packing, all sizes of pillows, and other similar materials for the space invaders to walk on during their journey. Be sure to turn out the lights and close the curtains. Give each child a flashlight and . . . four, three, two, one . . . BLAST OFF!

If time allows, have some of the children make space suits by painting paper bags and cutting out circles for their eyes and a rectangle for their mouth. Attach a string to the bottom of the bag with a small cardboard "microphone" at the end to be used for talking to other astronauts and to the mother ship. Let the children decorate their space suits with sequins, glitter, Styrofoam balls, etc. — the more outrageous the better.

Have other children become "martians" by painting their paper bags green and attaching antennae made from straws wrapped in foil. Who knows? The astronauts and martians may join forces!

Materials: sheets, blankets, chairs, tables, foil, balloons, flashlights, egg cartons, Styrofoam packing, pillows; paper bags, paint, string, cardboard, straws, decorative supplies (optional)

"That's one small step for man, one giant leap for mankind."

Neil A. Armstrong

String Detectives

Unwind a ball of string or yarn all around the room, up and down, through and between things until there is a trail of string everywhere! Choose one child as the "detective" and give him or her one clue — a spool threaded on the beginning of the string. The detective "ties up the case" by pushing the spool to the other end of the string. Don't forget the reward!

Materials: spool or large bead, ball of string or yarn, reward

"Success does for living what sunshine does for stained glass."

Bob Talbert

Ugly Bug Ball

Have the children make invitations for everyone to come to the "Ugly Bug Ball." Set a time and be sure everyone is in costume. Use throw-aways or odds and ends to make ugly bug outfits. Put out paste and have scissors ready for whatever the children create. (Let costumes dry for at least a day.) The party begins when everyone is dressed as an ugly bug. Find a partner and waltz the day away.

Song by Burl Ives:

"Gotta crawl, gotta crawl, gotta crawl
To the Ugly Bug Ball, to the ball, to the ball.

Materials: paper and crayons for invitations, egg cartons, paper plates, styrofoam packing balls, lids, paper bags, foil, cardboard tubes, old socks, nylons, spoons, clothespins, paint, etc.

"Imagination wanders far afield."

Young

Unbirthday Party

Plan an unbirthday party! Everyone who isn't having a birthday is invited. The children make invitations, blow up balloons and hang streamers. Together make a gift for the whole group — maybe a papier mache pinata, a book about birthdays, a birdfeeder, or a planted seed in a pot. Give each child an apple with a candle on the top. Everyone sings "Happy Birthday" and blows out his or her own candle. Play party games or have relay races.

The children can also make unbirthday cards to give to someone else. Use yarn, paper, glue, macaroni, felt, crayons, and scissors to create a personal greeting. When the children exchange cards, they feel the joy of giving and receiving something handmade and personal.

*This is an enjoyable activity for everyone, especially when it's raining outside and the holidays are over. Be sure to involve the children in the planning of the unbirthday party. It will make their own birthdays more meaningful.

Materials: paper, crayons and art materials for making invitations, balloons and party decorations, gift-making materials, candles, games (optional)

"Incongruity is the mainspring of laughter."

Max Beerbohm

Rain Check

On those occasions when there isn't time to tell that special story, give that lesson in bike-riding, or that chance to visit a friend, give a "rain check" for later. The children will know that the special time will come again soon.

*Children often want immediate attention. Rain checks may help them understand that occasionally a special time must be delayed.

Materials: paper, pen

"Life is a series of experiences, each one of which makes us bigger, even though sometimes it is hard to realize this."

Henry Ford